EXTREME CAREERS™

U.S. AIR MARSHALS

Matthew Broyles

rosen publishing's
rosen
central®

New York

This book is dedicated to Pete Waller, with fondest regards

Published in 2007 by The Rosen Publishing Group, Inc.
29 East 21st Street, New York, NY 10010

Library of Congress Cataloging-in-Publication Data

Broyles, Matthew.
U.S. air marshals / Matthew Broyles. — 1st ed.
p. cm. — (Extreme careers)
Includes bibliographical references and index.
ISBN-13: 978-1-4042-0942-8
ISBN-10: 1-4042-0942-5 (library binding)
1. Transportation—United States—Safety measures—Juvenile literature.
2. Airports—Security measures—United States—Juvenile literature.
I. Title.
HE194.5.U6B76 2007
363.28'76—dc22

                                        2006020733

Manufactured in the United States of America

On the cover: Air marshals train for an in-flight terrorist emergency in this simulation exercise.

Contents

Introduction

If you are flying on a commercial airplane, no matter where you're going, no matter what airline you choose, no matter what time of day it is, there is a good chance that you are riding with an air marshal. Air marshals are undercover federal law enforcement officers charged with protecting the lives of passengers and preventing hijackings, bombings, and other kinds of terrorist attacks. You probably won't spot them. They're trained to blend in with other passengers, and their disguises can range from businessperson to tourist to college student. Air marshals are everywhere, and they are some of the most highly skilled and courageous law enforcement and antiterrorist personnel the United States government employs.

For those with the ability, the courage, and the ambition, a career as an air marshal can be exciting and

Thousands of passengers move through U.S. airports every day. U.S. air marshals look at each of them as a potential terrorist.

rewarding. It can allow you to protect innocent civilians from the threat of terrorism in the skies. However, it is a career that is not for the faint of heart. Being an air marshal requires sacrifice, bravery, discipline, and dedication. This book will give you the information you need to decide if a career as an air marshal is right for you.

A New Threat in the Skies

The first bombing on a U.S. civilian airliner took place in 1955, when a man named Jack Graham hid a bomb in his mother's luggage. The bomb exploded and killed all forty-four people aboard the plane. Though Graham's aim was only to collect his mother's life insurance policy, others would later find different—often political—uses for acts of violence in the air.

Hijacking: A Growing Problem

In 1958, Communist forces under the command of revolutionary leader Fidel Castro took control of the small Caribbean island nation of Cuba. Soon, anti-Castro individuals began hijacking, or taking forcible control of, Cuban planes, attempting to divert them to the United States. Shortly thereafter, in 1961, pro-Castro Cuban exiles began hijacking U.S. planes and diverting them to Cuba.

All of this caused President John F. Kennedy to launch the first U.S. sky marshal program to put an end to the hijackings. In 1961, Kennedy signed a law stating that hijacking (also called "air piracy") was now punishable by death. It was the job of the sky marshals to apprehend hijackers and bring them to justice. However, hijackings were still very rare in the mid-1960s, and the number of sky marshals was kept very low. But in 1968, all of that changed.

On February 9, 1968, a U.S. Marine stationed in South Vietnam unsuccessfully attempted to hijack a military flight out of the country. Similar hijackings followed, and hijacking soon became an epidemic. The following year brought the highest number of U.S. hijackings ever. In October 1969, a marine named Raphael Minichiello went AWOL (absent without leave, or permission), hijacked a flight out of Los Angeles, California, and diverted it to Rome, Italy. This was the first time an airliner had been diverted over such a great distance. Ten days later, a fourteen-year-old boy, whose mother claimed he was influenced by Minichiello, attempted to hijack a flight in Cincinnati, Ohio. Alarmed by the increasing number of attacks, airlines began using metal detectors to screen passengers for weapons, but the midair assaults continued.

Some hijackings were intended to take individuals to foreign countries, but others were used to extort money or promote political agendas such as the freeing of Palestinian prisoners in Israel. In June 1970, a man named Arthur Barkley took control of a plane in Washington, D.C., demanding a $100 million ransom from the U.S. government. He was overpowered and the hijacking failed. In September 1970, two American planes and a Swiss plane were hijacked simultaneously and taken to an airstrip in Jordan, where they were destroyed by explosives after they were evacuated. As a result, President Richard Nixon announced in late 1970 that existing sky marshals were now to be armed, the better to stop hijackers in their tracks, before planes could be taken over and diverted.

The hijacking problem kept growing, however. On November 24, 1971, a man named D. B. Cooper hijacked a plane in Portland, Oregon. He demanded a $200,000 ransom and two parachutes, with which he

In 1970, the Palestine Liberation Organization hijacked three airplanes and blew them up after first removing the passengers.

escaped. He was never found. This inspired others to try extortion hijackings, both in U.S. airspace and worldwide. Some were successful, though most were not.

By 1972, the sky marshal program had grown along with increasingly sophisticated airport security methods to detect weapons. The number of hijackings dropped dramatically. As a result, in 1974, the number of sky marshals was reduced. For more than a decade, it seemed that America's airliners were once again safe.

The hijacking of TWA Flight 847 in 1985 was one of the chief incidents that led to the expansion of the air marshal program under President Ronald Reagan.

That all changed in June 1985. On board TWA Flight 847 from Athens, Greece, two Lebanese terrorists succeeded in diverting the flight to Beirut, Lebanon, where additional hijackers joined them for a two-week stand-off. By the time it was over, the terrorists had killed a U.S. Navy diver named Robert Stetham, who happened to be a passenger on the flight.

This tragic event, coinciding with an increase in terrorist acts throughout the Middle East, led President Ronald Reagan to expand the sky marshal program, now called the air marshal program. Air marshals were placed on international flights of U.S. airliners, and the program grew to include approximately 400 marshals by 1987.

But by the mid-1990s, terror in the skies had again become rare. Gradually, the program was reduced in size, until at last it employed only thirty-three marshals by September 2001.

September 11

On the morning of September 11, 2001, the most horrific hijacking in U.S. history was carried out by nineteen terrorists on board four U.S. planes. The planes were taken over and crashed into the World Trade Center in New York City, the Pentagon in Arlington, Virginia, and a field near Shanksville, Pennsylvania. The hijackers were armed only with box cutters, simple razor blades encased in metal sheaths. There are few reliable accounts of exactly how the attacks took place, mostly drawn from cell phone calls from passengers during the hijackings. Based on this information, it is most often presumed that the terrorists waited until after takeoff, killed or injured the crews of each aircraft, took control of the cockpits, and piloted the airplanes toward their targets.

More than 3,000 people were killed in the attacks (mostly in the collapse of the Twin Towers of the World Trade Center), many more wounded, and the country was thrown into a state of turmoil and panic. All passenger aircraft in the United States were grounded for several days, while the government assessed the air security situation.

Several solutions were proposed and implemented. The most important of these were initiatives to improve airport security screening, require armored and locked cockpit doors to shield pilots from attack,

Airport security cameras show two of the September 11, 2001, hijackers going through security, including the alleged ringleader, Mohammed Atta.

and increase the tracking of suspected terrorists both in the United States and abroad. It turned out that many of the individuals later identified as the nineteen hijackers were known to U.S. intelligence agencies. Several had taken flying lessons in American flight schools. They had aroused suspicion and were reported to the authorities because some of them expressed an interest in learning how to fly, but not how to take off and land. However, communication between the nation's main intelligence agencies—the Federal Bureau of Investigation (FBI) and the Central Intelligence Agency (CIA)—was poor. They didn't share information they had gathered and tips they had received on the suspicious flight students. There was also no efficient, accessible way for airline security personnel to know which passengers might be potential threats. These security personnel were employed by the airlines themselves, were often paid close to minimum wage, and had no clearance to receive relevant information from agencies such as the FBI.

In the wake of what came to be known simply as 9/11, whole airports were redesigned to satisfy the new security requirements. Only ticketed passengers were allowed to proceed to the gates. In some cases, only ticketed passengers were allowed in the terminals themselves, which were now fortified with security checkpoints at all entrances and staffed by carefully screened federal employees. The federal government set up no-fly lists, based on the suspicious activities of individuals reported to the FBI and CIA. Government agents were given greater authority to place wiretaps on the telephones of American citizens and to monitor their Internet activity, including e-mail.

A prototype device that scans shoes for explosives is tested in San Francisco, California, in 2005.

Many of these new security measures were authorized by the USA PATRIOT Act, passed by Congress in October 2001. The fact that the federal government was allowed to monitor the private communications and activities of citizens remains controversial. For example, the government has ordered phone and Internet companies to hand over records of their customers' activity. Even book purchases or library loans can be monitored by the government now. Many Americans feel their civil liberties—a fundamental cornerstone of the country's democracy—have been compromised or even trampled in the name of national security.

As a part of this drive for greater security, the government once again turned to the air marshal program, which it now renamed the Federal Air Marshal Service (FAMS). By November 17, 2001, the Aviation and Transportation Security Act (ATSA) was passed, which greatly increased the number of air marshals in active duty. The program was eventually placed under the command of the newly formed Department of Homeland Security (DHS), since FAMS's mission and that of the DHS are the same—protecting the United States from attack.

The Screening Process

Because of the job's importance to the national security of the United States and the safety of its citizens, federal air marshal (FAM) candidates are screened thoroughly. Thousands of air marshal hopefuls apply each year, but only a few are chosen. They are usually drawn from the military, from law enforcement, or straight out of college. All possess skills desired by the Federal Air Marshal Service, depending on its needs at that time. But the screening process is designed to reveal to federal recruiters more than a candidate's qualifications. It also gives them insight into which of the thousands of applicants has the right stuff for this demanding and unique job.

Before applying, there are a few things you should know right off the bat about the job requirements:

- Candidates must be between twenty-one and thirty-seven years old. The reason for the cutoff at age thirty-seven is that the required retirement age of gun-carrying federal employees is fifty-seven. If someone becomes an air marshal at age thirty-seven, they can work the twenty years necessary to earn a full pension.

- All candidates must be American citizens, either born in the United States or naturalized prior to applying.

- A high school diploma is required. College degrees are preferred, but not absolutely necessary. A military background or local law enforcement experience is extremely helpful, though not required. A computer science degree or fluency in one or more foreign languages can be just as valuable in getting in the door.

If you meet these basic requirements, the next step is to visit www.usajobs.opm.gov to find the application information for the Federal Air Marshal Service. It is listed under the Department of Homeland Security and

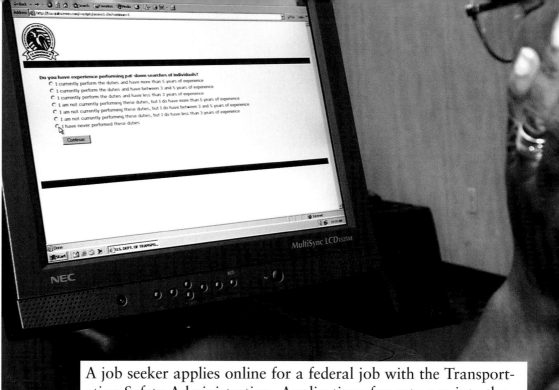

A job seeker applies online for a federal job with the Transportation Safety Administration. Applications for entrance into the
Federal Air Marshal Service can be found on both the TSA and
the Department of Homeland Security Web sites.

the Transportation Safety Administration (TSA). Honesty
is important when filling out the application, since all
details you provide will be scrutinized and verified.

After the Application

Upon receiving and reviewing your application, the TSA
will ask you to fill out a questionnaire. This form will
test your writing skills, among other things. Effective

communication is a major part of an air marshal's job. When you're the lone voice of authority during a crisis high in the sky, every word counts.

Should your questionnaire pass evaluation, the next step is a panel interview at one of the twenty-one FAM offices across the country. You will face a room full of air marshals, supervisors, and special agents, all asking a wide variety of tough questions to determine if you are potential air marshal material. After the interview, the panel will decide whether you move on to the next step—the physical fitness assessment test.

It's important to remember that air marshals are law enforcement officers, just like police or FBI agents. So it's vital that FAMs are in peak physical shape, ready to spring into action at the first sign of trouble. The physical fitness assessment test the TSA administers is rigorous, involving large numbers of push-ups, sit-ups, and long-distance running. A thorough medical exam is also given, to uncover any conditions that may one day affect your ability to perform your job. Since most FAMs stay on for at least twenty years, the exam administrators are thinking about applicants' long-term health.

Physical fitness is essential for air marshal candidates. Whether or not the air marshal is faster and stronger than the terrorists may determine the outcome of a hijacking.

An air marshal's mental health is as important as his or her physical health. An extensive psychological test is given to all FAM candidates. Dealing with threatening and probably armed terrorists in a plane full of terrified civilians demands a clear head and a solid constitution. Losing your composure is not an option.

Having cleared all these hurdles, the only remaining obstacle for a FAM candidate is the background check in which any arrests, drug use, involvement in outlawed or

Marshals Gone Wrong

As thorough as FAM background checks are, they can't always accurately predict future behavior. In February 2006, two Houston-based air marshals faced charges of drug smuggling. One of the men, Shawn Ray Nguyen, had received 15 kilograms (31 pounds) of cocaine and $15,000 at his home and had promised to take the drugs on a plane, according to prosecutors. However, the man he and fellow FAM Burlie Sholar made the deal with turned out to be a government agent who turned them in. In addition, Nguyen is alleged to have smuggled money, forged government documents, and $25,000 worth of narcotics on a flight in December 2005. During the trial of the two air marshals, evidence came to light that perhaps more FAMs could be involved. They accepted a plea bargain and were sentenced to seven- and nine-year prison terms.

suspicious organizations, credit problems, or other evidence of unstable or illegal activity is gathered and examined. In an interview with the author, Dave Adams, the special agent in charge of public affairs for the Federal Air Marshal Service, had some words for young people about keeping their record clean: "When you think having a little drug possession offense or other misdemeanor won't matter, think again. Every single infraction on your record will be noted and may keep you from getting this job."

A clean background check clears the way for the FAM candidate to receive top-secret clearance from the U.S. government. The information an air marshal receives in the course of his or her duties often comes from the highest levels of the federal government. This is why you'll almost never know if you're talking to an air marshal. The more anonymous the FAM, the safer the information he or she possesses remains. Upon receiving their top-secret clearance, candidates are ready to begin their training. In the words of FAM agent Adams, it's not boot camp, "but it's pretty close."

Air Marshal Training

The Federal Law Enforcement Training Center for the federal air marshal program is located in Artesia, New Mexico. It is the training facility used for many top-secret government agencies such as the CIA. Here, air marshal candidates have their physical, emotional, and mental limits put to the test. Obstacle courses, firearms training, and long hours of physical exertion await FAM trainees on a daily basis for seven long weeks.

That, however, is just the beginning. After the seven weeks spent in Artesia, the trainees who make it through head to Atlantic City, New Jersey, home of the federal air marshal academy. There, they go through a second seven-week period of intense training.

An important part of academy training involves firearms. The difficulty of firing weapons inside a long,

The Federal Law Enforcement Training Center in Artesia, New Mexico, is where air marshals and other high-level government agents, like CIA officers, are trained.

narrow, tube-shaped aircraft and possibly critically damaging the plane or hitting any innocent passengers means that the firearms training requirements for FAMs are among the strictest in the government.

Equally important are defensive measures that prevent weapons from being fired in the first place. Taking down a hijacker without endangering the lives of the other passengers is a tricky task and demands a wide knowledge of defensive techniques. The academy's experts ensure

Air marshal trainees practice shooting targets. In a narrow airplane cabin, accuracy is all-important.

that every FAM is well armed and defended, with a gun or without.

A little-known part of an air marshal's job is surveillance detection. Agent Adams told the author that "an air marshal's job starts the minute they leave their front door." On the highways, in stores, and around airports, any sign of suspicious activity will attract an air marshal's attention. FAMs have access to a secret wireless communication system that connects them to federal and

Guns in the Air

The James Bond film *Goldfinger*, while entertaining, unfortunately started a popular myth. Those who see the film may believe that if a bullet shoots through the skin of an aircraft, the cabin will depressurize. In reality, the pumps and compressors that pressurize an airplane cabin will safely deal with a few small bullet holes. Furthermore, air marshals normally use Charter Arms .44 Special Bulldog revolvers that fire Glaser Safety Slugs, which most likely would not pierce the walls of the cabin in the first place. FAMs are also trained to hit hijackers in the torso, so that the bullet would stay in the body rather than continue on to cause damage elsewhere in the plane. The real danger comes not from bullets going through the plane's walls, but into its electrical and hydraulic wiring. This is the primary reason why air marshals are among the best marksmen in law enforcement.

local law enforcement. They can be in touch with these law enforcement agents and feed them information about suspicious persons and activities no matter where they happen to be. If an air marshal can help stop terrorists before they even reach the airport or get on a plane,

their job will be made that much easier. The academy trains FAMs in the detection of threats wherever they may present themselves, not just in the sky.

If a candidate makes it through the fourteen-week period of intense training in New Mexico and New Jersey,

In this training simulation, an air marshal *(far left)* moves to fire on a hijacker who is holding a knife to the throat of a flight crew member.

supervisors will most likely make a recommendation for awarding him or her the position of air marshal.

The training doesn't stop there, however. At least twenty days per year, even established and long-serving FAMs must train at one of the field offices throughout the country. These offices have many of the same training facilities as the academy in Atlantic City, including an aircraft cabin simulator where FAMs use live ammunition to keep up their firearms skills in terrorist attack scenarios. Air marshals must keep their skills sharp for that one split second when their services might be required. If air marshals fail to react in time, their lives are in every bit as much danger as those around them in the air. And if an air marshal goes down, the passengers are left undefended, and their chances of surviving unharmed are reduced dramatically.

A Typical Day on the Job

Let's suppose you've passed all the tests and completed your training, and you're now a newly minted federal air marshal. What would your typical workweek be like?

Actually, you might not have any typical weeks. Your schedule would seldom be the same from month to month, since unpredictability is part of what makes air marshals effective. You would receive your schedule for the month twenty-eight days in advance, just to make sure there were no conflicts. After all, even air marshals have personal lives, though the schedule requirements of the job make some difficult demands on agents' home life and relationships.

Some of your days would involve working in your local field office. Approximately ten of the forty hours air marshals work each week are spent dealing with

Passengers approach Seattle on a ferry. Air marshals on their way to work keep an eye out for suspicious activity on all kinds of transportation, including ferries.

paperwork. Part of that time would also be spent training, or perhaps taking part in panel interviews of air marshal candidates.

But most days, you would get up at an appropriate time to catch whatever flight you were assigned to take that day. You might be leaving from your home, or you might be in a hotel where you stayed after taking a flight the previous day to another city. Air marshals' work can take them around the country or around the world. You might wake up in New York and go to sleep in Paris, Tokyo, or Jerusalem.

Your wardrobe may change often. Again, unpredictability is a key element in your job. If a terrorist is flying a given route several times to scout for air marshals, he may not think that the biker he saw one day was the college professor he saw another day, though they are one and the same person.

As Agent Adams says, your job would begin as soon as you leave your front door. The airport is not the only place where terrorists operate, so you would keep your eyes peeled through the course of the day for any suspicious activity. Air marshals travel so often that they see many of the

Air marshals are on alert for suspicious activity everywhere they go.

same places a lot. They become so familiar with their surroundings that they can even tell whether a newspaper stand is out of place or an unmarked delivery truck is parked for an unusual length of time. If you did see something out of the ordinary, you would use your secure, top-secret wireless device to report the activity to local or federal law enforcement authorities.

Upon reaching the airport, your observation of the surroundings would intensify. Air marshals keep a watchful eye out for passengers behaving in strange or secretive ways, well before the airplane begins to board. For example, you might notice someone with an over-sized coat on in the middle of August or someone with baggy pants stained with oil that may be leaking from an explosive device. You would decide to keep an eye on that person and continue to study his or her behavior in the passenger lounge. Air marshals are the official law enforcement arm of the TSA, so if any action is taken against suspected terrorists in U.S. airports, FAMs will be central to the response.

Eventually, you would board the aircraft along with the other passengers. Again, you would pay close attention to the behavior of those getting on the plane. Your training

Since 9/11, non-ticketed people can no longer greet or send off passengers in the terminal. Only ticketed passengers may occupy the terminal, after first passing through security.

would give you insight into who might pose a potential threat, and you would begin planning the best response should that threat materialize.

Once the plane is in the air, your surveillance continues for the duration of the flight. The vast majority of flights are uneventful, but you have been trained for the one that isn't. And often, it can be difficult to determine the right course of action, especially when a split-second decision, made under extreme pressure, is required.

At the end of your week as a federal air marshal, you would write reports of events that occurred during the flights you took. Even the smallest occurrence might ring a bell with another agency such as the FBI or CIA, who could be investigating someone that an air marshal came into contact with on an airplane.

Career Advancement and Retirement

If you were to remain an air marshal long enough and do a good enough job, you could move up the chain of command and even become the director of the agency. However, some air marshals eventually move to other government defense agencies, using their air marshal experience as a springboard. Federal Air Marshal Service special agent David Adams himself started as a local policeman, moved to the Secret Service for twenty years, then worked in the Immigration and Naturalization Service for six and a half years before becoming a federal air marshal.

After twenty years in the Federal Air Marshal Service, you would have the opportunity to retire with a full pension. The program also offers a retirement savings plan similar to a 401(k) and many other benefits. But retirement doesn't necessarily mean you have to stop working. Many federal employees move into other fields (often related to security or law enforcement) while collecting their pension, increasing their earnings as long as they choose to keep working.

Life or Death Decisions

Air marshals can suddenly find themselves thrown into situations in which they must make split-second life or death decisions, based upon a very small amount of available information and almost no time to process it. It isn't always obvious who the bad guys are on a plane, or even if there are any truly bad guys present, as opposed to simply poorly behaved passengers. In fact, of the forty passengers arrested by air marshals since the terrorist acts of September 11, 2001, none have been linked to terrorist activity or organizations. Yet it only takes one terrorist to create a national catastrophe, and that is why air marshals, their sharply honed instincts, and their best judgment are required.

The Case of Rigo Alpizar

On December 7, 2005, a man named Rigo Alpizar boarded American Airlines Flight 924 in Miami, Florida, bound for Orlando. He had just taken a flight to Miami from Ecuador. A passenger on that flight recalled him being extremely agitated.

Rigo Alpizar's erratic behavior on a plane in Miami led to his shooting death at the hands of federal air marshals.

According to the accounts of one passenger and the air marshals on the flight, Alpizar, while waiting for the plane to depart Miami, began saying, "I've got to get off, I've got to get off." Many other passengers recall him running down the aisle of the plane, clutching his bag and heading for the exit, followed by a man in a Hawaiian shirt. That man turned out to be a federal air marshal.

When Alpizar ran off the plane and into the boarding bridge, he was confronted by two air marshals, one of whom was the agent who had been seated on the flight. The FAMs later reported that Alpizar had been shouting, "I have a bomb in my bag!" as he ran off the plane.

According to special agent David Adams, "They asked the gentleman, 'Drop your bag . . . Come to the ground . . . Police. Drop your bag.' He failed to comply with their commands, continued approaching the air marshals claiming he had a bomb in his bag. And then they ordered him again down to the ground. He didn't." (Quotes are from the CNN.com article "White House Backs Air Marshal's Actions.")

Adams says that Alpizar then reached into his backpack, which had initially drawn attention because he wore it over his chest rather than on his back. At that point, the air marshals fired several shots, killing Alpizar. This was the first time that any FAM had fired a shot in the line of duty. As it turned out, Alpizar did not have a bomb in his bag and was, in fact, suffering from bipolar disorder. This condition can lead to episodes of manic behavior and extreme depression, and requires medication he did not have with him at the time.

Second-Guessing the Air Marshals

There has been debate in the press and within Congress as to whether the FAMs acted correctly in the Alpizar incident, though the White House publicly supported their actions. Since 9/11, only one other incident resulted in air marshals drawing their weapons. That happened in August 2002, when two agents on a Delta flight to Philadelphia, Pennsylvania, had to restrain an unruly passenger. The situation got very tense, according to passengers, since one of the FAMs reportedly held the entire coach section at gunpoint. One passenger described it as a high-altitude version of *Rambo*.

There have also been cases in which air marshals were harassed by passengers. An Illinois businessman stood up during one flight and pointed out passengers he believed to be air marshals. A woman on a flight preparing to depart Pittsburgh, Pennsylvania, reportedly had too much to drink. She was hauled off the plane before takeoff for talking about the plane exploding. She then attempted to choke an air marshal who was trying to calm her down.

The Alpizar case and these other incidents demonstrate how complicated and dangerous onboard situations can get when the nature of the threat is unclear. However, the reason the FAM program was expanded in 2001 was to respond to a much clearer, unambiguous threat: Al Qaeda, the terrorist organization responsible for the 9/11 attacks and founded by terrorist mastermind and funder Osama bin Laden.

High-Altitude Counterterrorism

The events of September 11, 2001, might have gone very differently—perhaps even been prevented altogether—if there had been air marshals aboard the four flights that were hijacked that day. The nineteen hijackers were armed only with box cutters, whereas FAMs carry loaded pistols. And even if they were unable to use their guns for some reason, their self-defense training might have enabled them to take out the hijackers without harming any other passengers or the crew.

Another incident in which the presence of air marshals would have been useful occurred on December 22, 2001. That day, a twenty-eight-year-old British man named

Richard Reid boarded American Airlines Flight 93 leaving Paris, France, for Miami, Florida. He had attempted to take the same flight a day before but was stopped and questioned by French authorities because he was boarding without checked luggage. After extensive questioning, Reid was released too late to catch the flight but was allowed to take one the following day.

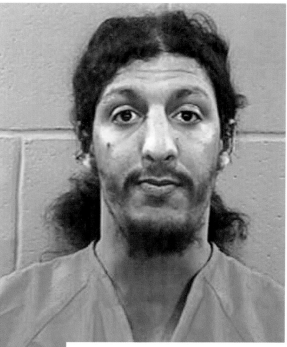

Richard Reid attempted to blow up an airplane using a bomb hidden in his shoe.

As the plane flew over the Atlantic Ocean, Reid lit a match. When a passing flight attendant confronted him, he blew it out and placed it in his mouth. The attendant left to inform the captain of the incident and returned to find Reid bent over, with another match held to the tongue of his shoe. Suddenly, she noticed a wire sticking out of the top of the shoe. She quickly

Richard Reid's shoes contained enough plastic explosives to blow a hole in the side of the airplane.

moved to grab the sneaker, but Reid tossed her to the floor as she screamed for help.

A second flight attendant rushed to help, and Reid bit her on the thumb. The first attendant managed to throw water in his face, distracting him as surrounding passengers subdued him. Several took off their belts and strapped him into his seat. Two doctors happened to be on board. They used drugs from the plane's medical kit to sedate Reid until the flight could be escorted by U.S. fighter jets to Logan Airport in Boston, Massachusetts.

Fortunately, the passengers on the flight were able to stop Reid before he lit his shoe bomb, but they could just as easily have failed. Had an air marshal been on board, the incident may have been stopped at the first sign of trouble, such as the lighting of the match. It is exactly these kinds of situations that call for a trained air marshal to act quickly to defuse threats. In response to Reid's attempted bombing, airports now require passengers to remove their shoes for inspection before boarding aircraft. Still, bombs can take many forms, and FAMs have to be on the lookout for creative terrorists who have placed explosives in unexpected places. As the foiled airliner bomb plot of August 2006 revealed, terrorists are even trying to smuggle liquid explosives on board in common objects such as water bottles and lotion jars.

Since 9/11, there have been very few reports of midair incidents involving air marshals. As Special Agent David Adams told the author, "We like to think that the lack of interesting or exciting stories involving air marshals means that we're doing our job right." Still, the agency is very secretive, and it's entirely possible that many plots have been stopped early enough that the press never found out about them. Of course, this would be a further and even more encouraging indication that the FAMS is doing its job right.

Trouble Ahead?

Despite the service's recent expansion, the future of the air marshals remains cloudy. Occasionally, a FAM will

U.S. marshals on patrol at Miami International Airport, two days after 9/11. At the time of the attacks, the air marshal program was not large enough to cope with the new terrorist threat.

come forward to offer criticism of the way the program is being run.

One FAM, who spoke anonymously for a *Vanity Fair* magazine article in February 2006, detailed how a terrorist might think: "I get on a plane, let's say an L.A.-to-JFK flight, six hours, and I already know where [the marshals] are sitting. I know what they look like. I watched them in the airport—they got paraded by the passengers . . . Eventually, one of them has got to go to the bathroom, right? So the partner goes into the bathroom, and I come up on the guy—one good, swift punch into the carotid artery will render him unconscious. Then I take his gun and wait for his partner to get out of the lav and shoot him. Now I've got two weapons." According to the article, a pilot for a major airline said the question that needs to be asked is, "Are we really safer with them or without them?"

The problems that the anonymous air marshal details above stem from the fact that, at present, air marshals' cover can be blown by the procedures they have to use while boarding. FAMs have to present their very large badges at the ticket counter, again at the metal detectors, and yet again at the gate. In addition, at least one air marshal in a team boards before anyone else, including first-class passengers. The reason is sound—communication with the pilot and crew and inspecting the plane for suspicious items. But all of this conspicuous badge-flashing and early boarding can compromise the identities of air marshals, especially if they are being observed by keen-eyed terrorists. Indeed, would-be terrorists are probably on the lookout for air marshals every bit as vigilantly as air marshals are trying to identify terrorists.

Another stumbling block to the air marshals fulfilling their duties is the FAMS organization itself. Since 2004, tensions between then-FAMS director Thomas Quinn and a large number of air marshals had been steadily climbing toward the boiling point, eventually resulting in Quinn's resignation in February 2006. Quinn, a Secret Service veteran like Agent Adams, was accused of poorly managing his employees and treating them "like kinder-gartners," according to at least one air marshal. He was replaced by Dana Brown, a former police officer, Secret Service agent, and chief of staff of FAMS.

One of the biggest arguments grew out of the agency's dress code, instituted by Quinn. Per a memo in December 2004, agents were directed to wear sports coats, buttoned shirts with collars, and neatly pressed slacks with leather shoes. Such relatively formal attire, coupled with the already described pre-boarding procedures, threatened to make air marshals incredibly conspicuous. This alarmed many FAMs, who then complained.

Interviewed in *Vanity Fair*, Agent Adams explained the service's position, arguing that if an air marshal was dressed in shabby clothes, other passengers wouldn't follow his orders in the event of a crisis. The disagreement reached such a state that Congress itself directed the service to ease up on the restrictions, the better to protect the air marshals' identities. As of September 1, 2006, the marshals were allowed to dress as they wished.

Agents who criticize FAMS methods and policies are often fired, leading to even more discontent among air marshals. Many were reportedly ready to quit if Quinn was not replaced. Former Homeland Security inspector general Clark Kent Ervin issued several official criticisms of the department, leading to his dismissal by the White House. "The attitude I got at the department time and again," Ervin told *Vanity Fair*, "was, 'We don't want to hear bad news . . . Either ignore the problem or deny it exists, or minimize it, or ridicule it, or claim it has already been fixed and our reports are old news."

Government agencies, including the Federal Air Marshal Service and its predecessors, have faced these sorts of internal disagreements and tensions before. Generally, they have come out better for it. With any luck, the current turmoil will make the service stronger and better able to confront the threats faced by the United States.

A U.S. marshal patrols Reagan International Airport in Washington, D.C., in October 2001. Due to its proximity to the White House, Congress, and other vital federal government locations, Reagan International was the last airport to reopen after the 9/11 attacks.

A Few Good Marshals

A federal air marshal's job is incredibly demanding and dangerous, and the anonymity it requires leaves no room for seeking glory. But for those who have the desire to keep innocent people safe from terrorist attacks, it is an amazing opportunity to have a major impact on the lives of American citizens.

Like other federal law enforcement and intelligence agents, air marshals do their job in secrecy and with pinpoint precision. Lives are at stake, and an ordinary day can become extraordinary in a matter of seconds. In those seconds, training and alertness come together to stop a potentially deadly attack. As the events of September 11, 2001, negatively demonstrate, the actions of a very few can affect a whole nation. The air marshals exist to show how one or two individuals can positively affect the lives of many and protect the well-being of the country.

Glossary

cabin The enclosed space inside an aircraft that the passengers and crew occupy during flight.

cockpit The space inside the cabin set apart for the pilot and copilot.

extort To demand and receive money by threatening someone.

hijack To take control of a vehicle by force.

marksman A person skilled at shooting a target. The female version of this is called a markswoman.

questionnaire A form containing a set of questions designed to establish one's opinions about something or one's qualifications for a given task or job.

ransom The money received through extortion, kidnapping, or hostage-taking.

screening In the case of airline security, the process used to detect weapons in luggage. In the case of air marshal recruitment, the process used to select qualified candidates from among all those who apply for the job.

surveillance Close observation of a person or group.

terrorism The unlawful use of violence, usually against civilians, to force political or social change or put forth a political agenda.

wiretap A concealed listening device used to monitor communication, usually installed on telephones.

For More Information

Central Intelligence Agency (CIA)
Office of Public Affairs
Washington, DC 20505
(703) 482-0623
Web site: http://www.cia.gov

Federal Air Marshal Association
Corporate Headquarters
8020 South Las Vegas Boulevard
Las Vegas, NV 89123
Web site: http://www.famaonline.com/

Federal Aviation Administration
800 Independence Avenue SW
Washington, DC 20591

(866) TELL-FAA (835-5322)
Web site: http://www.faa.gov

Federal Bureau of Investigation (FBI)
J. Edgar Hoover Building
935 Pennsylvania Avenue NW
Washington, DC 20535-0001
(202) 324-3000
Web site: http://www.fbi.gov

National Transportation Library
Bureau of Transportation Statistics
U.S. Department of Transportation
400 Seventh Street SW
Washington, DC 20590
(800) 853-1351
Web site: http://ntl.bts.gov

Transportation Security Administration
601 South 12th Street
Arlington, VA 22202
(866) 289-9673
Web site: http://www.tsa.gov/public/index.jsp

U.S. Department of Homeland Security

Washington, DC 20528
(202) 282-8000
Web site: http://www.dhs.gov/dhspublic/

U.S. Department of Transportation

400 7th Street SW
Washington, DC 20590
(202) 366-4000
www.dot.gov/

Web Sites

Due to the changing nature of Internet links, Rosen Publishing has developed an online list of Web sites related to the subject of this book. This site is updated regularly. Please use this link to access the list:

http://www.rosenlinks.com/ec/usam

For Further Reading

Abrams, Norman. *Anti-Terrorism and Criminal Enforcement.* Belmont, CA: Thomson/West, 2005.

Johnson, Loch K. *Bombs, Bugs, Drugs, and Thugs: Intelligence and America's Quest for Security.* New York, NY: New York University Press, 2002.

Lesser, Ian O., et al. *Countering the New Terrorism.* Santa Monica, CA: RAND Corp., 1999.

National Commission on Terrorist Attacks. *The 9/11 Commission Report: Final Report of the National Commission on Terrorist Attacks Upon the United States.* New York, NY: W. W. Norton and Co., 2004.

Posner, Richard A. *Preventing Surprise Attacks: Intelligence Reform in the Wake of 9/11.* Lanham, MD: Rowman and Littlefield Publishers, Inc., 2005.

Sweet, Kathleen M. *Aviation and Airport Security: Terrorism and Safety Concerns.* Upper Saddle River, NJ: Prentice Hall, 2003.

White, Jonathan R. *Terrorism and Homeland Security.* Belmont, CA: Wadsworth Publishing, 2005.

Zellan, Jennifer, ed. *Aviation Security: Current Issues and Developments.* Hauppauge, NY: Nova Science Publishers, 2003.

Bibliography

Abrams, Norman. *Anti-Terrorism and Criminal Enforcement*. Belmont, CA: Thomson/West, 2005.

Adams, Dave. Interview by author. April 2006.

Ahlers, Mike M. "Ridge: 'Modest' Decline in Federal Air Marshals." CNN.com. March 4, 2004. Retrieved February 2006 (http://www.cnn.com/2004/TRAVEL/03/04/air.marshals.cut/index.html).

"Air Marshals Taught to Be Risk Averse." CNN.com. December 8, 2005. Retrieved March 2006 (http://www.cnn.com/2005/US/12/07/air.marshal/index.html).

Arena, Kelli, and Kevin Bohn. "Air Marshals Face Smuggling Charges." CNN.com. February 14, 2006. Retrieved February 2006 (http://www.cnn.com/2006LAW/02/13/marshals.cocaine/index.html).

Bevelacqua, Armando S. *Terrorism Handbook for Operational Responders.* 2nd ed. Belmont, CA: Thomson Delmar Learning, 2003.

Brown, Jim. "Air Marshals: Utilizing Law Enforcement Officers on Airplanes." *Law & Order.* December 31, 2001.

"Explosives, Wires Found in Sneakers: Man Charged with Assaulting Flight Crew in Scuffle." *Milwaukee Journal-Sentinel.* December 23, 2001.

Gooding, Richard. "Air Marshals: Are We Safer with Them or Without Them?" *Vanity Fair.* February 2006.

Heymann, Philip B. *Terrorism, Freedom, and Security: Winning Without War.* Cambridge, MA: MIT Press, 2004.

Hudson, Audrey. "Air Marshals Wait for New Director." *Washington Times.* January 19, 2006.

Posner, Richard A. *Preventing Surprise Attacks: Intelligence Reform in the Wake of 9/11.* Lanham, MD: Rowman and Littlefield Publishers, Inc., 2005.

Report to Congressional Requesters. *Aviation Security: Federal Air Marshal Service Is Addressing Challenges of Its Expanded Mission and Workforce, but Additional Actions Needed.* Washington, DC: General Accounting Office. December 1, 2003.

Rice, Harvey. "Other Air Marshals Implicated." *Houston Chronicle.* February 16, 2006.

Thompson, Leroy. "Air Marshals in Training." *Guns & Ammo.* Retrieved February 2006 (http://www.gunsandammomag.com/ga_handguns/air_marshalls).

"Timeline: The Shoe Bomber Case." CNN.com. January 7, 2002. Retrieved February 2006 (http://archives.cnn.com/2002/US/01/07/reid.timeline/index.html).

"White House Backs Air Marshals' Actions." CNN.com. December 9, 2005. Retrieved February 2006 (http://www.cnn.com/2005/US/12/08/airplane.gunshot/index.html).

Index

About the Author

Matthew Broyles is a writer living in Texas. In the course of researching this book and interviewing a special agent in the Federal Air Marshal Service, Broyles gained special insight into the workings of the service and the unique requirements of the job. He also gained a deep respect and appreciation for the men and women who keep our skies safe.

Photo Credits